Sydney Clair

A GIRL 'N GRACE IN THE 1960s

PAM DAVIS

with KATHY BUCHANAN

Authentic

COLORADO SPRINGS · MILTON KEYNES · HYDERABAD

Authentic Publishing
We welcome your questions and comments.

USA   1820 Jet Stream Drive, Colorado Springs, CO 80921 www.authenticbooks.com
UK   9 Holdom Avenue, Bletchley, Milton Keynes, Bucks, MK1 1QR
       www.authenticmedia.co.uk
India Logos Bhavan, Medchal Road, Jeedimetla Village, Secunderabad 500 055, A.P.

Sydney Clair: A Girl 'n Grace in the 1960s
ISBN-13: 978-1-934068-78-6
ISBN-10: 1-934068-78-0

10 09 08 / 6 5 4 3 2 1

Published in 2008 by Authentic

Scripture quotations are taken from the authorized King James Version. Public domain.

Author photo: Cliff Ranson, www.ransonphotography.com.
Images: © 2007 iStockphoto.com, and © 2007 JupiterImages Corporation

Illustrations: Monica Bucanelli
Cover/Interior design: Julia Ryan / www.DesignByJulia.com
Editorial team: Kathy Buchanan, Diane Stortz, Michaela Dodd, Dan Johnson

Printed in the United States of America

A catalog record is available from the Library of Congress.

CONTENTS

*To Luke Hawkins, my dad and friend
who showed me the Father's love.*

Welcome from the Author

Dear friends,

I am so pleased you are joining me as we journey through lives of girls in grace.

A Girl 'n Grace is a girl in whom the person of grace, Jesus Christ, lives. You'll notice there's a missing "I" and an apostrophe in its place. The Bible teaches that in order to live in a relationship with God one must surrender her life to Jesus. No longer do I live but rather it is Christ who lives in me as I live by faith in the Son of God (Galatians 2:20). A Girl 'n Grace is a girl who has surrendered her self-centered desires to the desires of Christ. In doing so, she discovers strength, satisfaction, and significance, which elevates her self-esteem and honors God.

Let this book aid you in discovering the desires of Jesus Christ, and may you, like these characters, proclaim, "I can through Christ."®

In his embrace,
Pam Davis
(Acts 20:24)

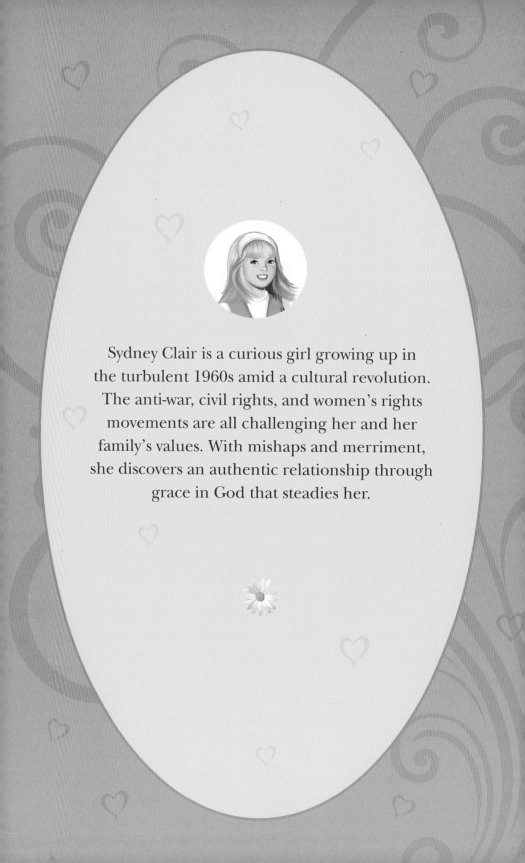

Sydney Clair is a curious girl growing up in the turbulent 1960s amid a cultural revolution. The anti-war, civil rights, and women's rights movements are all challenging her and her family's values. With mishaps and merriment, she discovers an authentic relationship through grace in God that steadies her.

Girls 'n Grace Place is a fun website where you can interact with the Girls 'n Grace characters.

You can . . .

join the free Reader's Club to take a quiz and win a prize! These heart-shaped icons in the book tell you there's a quiz question on the website.

participate with the Girls 'n Grace doll characters through a virtual experience and enjoy a wide range of activities: fashion, reader's club, travel, cooking, decorating, art, education, creating your own Girls 'n Grace magazine, and much more!

Visit the Girls 'n Grace characters at www.GirlsnGrace.com.

Chapter 1

The Promise

"That one looks like a piece of cake," said Vicky, pointing to a cloud overhead.

"Or a pretzel," said Ann.

"You're making me hungry," said Sydney Clair. With her friends she was taking a break from playing hopscotch in the afternoon sun. She could feel the damp grass beneath her as she lay under the shade of the large elm tree in her front yard. A quick summer rainstorm had done little to relieve the heat but much to fill the air with humidity.

"Hey, look!" said Ann. "A rainbow."

Sydney Clair twisted around on her stomach to see. Sure enough, a full rainbow arched across the sky. "Beautiful."

"We talked about rainbows in Sunday school," said Vicky. "God made the first one when Noah got out of the ark."

Sydney Clair knew the story. "It was about a promise, right?"

"Maybe the promise is there's a pot of gold at the end of it. Want to go see?" asked Ann.

"Not really," said Sydney Clair.

Ann sat up. "You've been so moody lately. You're usually up for anything. What's wrong?"

Sydney Clair thought Ann looked irritated with her.

"Yeah." Vicky pushed back her long ponytail over her shoulder. "You're really quiet. That's not like you at all."

Sydney Clair knew her friends were right. She *had* been grumpy lately. Mother said she was acting "down in the dumps," whatever that meant. She told Mother it was probably because the weather was so muggy, but in actuality she didn't know what was bothering her. In some strange way, she felt like she was missing something. She shrugged. "Maybe I'm just bored."

"A new dress," said Vicky, snapping her fingers. "That's what you need. When I'm feeling down, buying something new always cheers me up."

"I think I'd rather get a pogo stick," Ann said.

"Pogo sticks are not ladylike," argued Vicky.

Sydney Clair shrugged and went back to watching the clouds, only half listening to the conversation. She wondered what the clouds looked like to the crew of the *Gemini 4* space capsule. Just last month they had orbited the earth for four days!

"Look at that one!" Ann exclaimed, pointing. "A camel eating a giant hot dog!"

Sydney Clair looked where Ann was pointing. Then suddenly a furry head and a wet nose took over her view of the clouds. "Hi, puppy!" she laughed. "Where did you come from?"

A beautiful golden retriever looked sideways at Sydney Clair and flopped down next to her with his head on her lap.

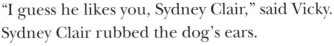

"I guess he likes you, Sydney Clair," said Vicky. Sydney Clair rubbed the dog's ears.

"Trouble! You bad dog! Get over here!" A panting middle-aged man carrying a leash jogged up behind the dog. "Don't bother these girls."

"He's not bothering us, sir," said Sydney Clair. "Is his name really Trouble?"

"Well, he gets himself into a lot of trouble, so the name stuck," the man explained. "Like now. He's *supposed* to be learning to walk beside me without a leash."

Sydney Clair laughed. Her gaze shifted from the dog to the flush-faced man. "I think he needs more work."

The man nodded. "I breed show dogs, but this one I might be stuck with."

"What's wrong with him? I think he's beautiful," said Sydney Clair.

"Pretty enough," said the man. "But look." He gripped the dog's jaw and pried his mouth open gently. Out flopped a wet pink tongue with a black spot in the center. "See? Some refer to this as a tongue fickle, but for a show dog it is considered a flaw."

Sydney Clair was thinking fast. "Would you be willing to sell him?"

The man laughed. "I'd love to sell him. I've even reduced his price to twenty-five dollars. But no takers." He raised an eyebrow. "You interested?"

Sydney Clair considered his question. Maybe this was what she needed. Maybe a dog would make her feel happy again. "I might be."

"Well, my place is on the corner of Fifth and Briar. Morgan's Dog Breeding. There's a sign out front. I'm Mr. Morgan."

Trouble pulled against the leash Mr. Morgan slipped around his neck.

Sydney Clair watched Mr. Morgan struggle to get Trouble back on the sidewalk. She shook her head. Sometimes she heard her parents talking about how hard it was to pay all their bills. She knew they wouldn't let her have a dog right now.

Ann stood up. "The rainbow is a sign."

Sydney Clair frowned. "What are you talking about?"

"The rainbow," Ann said. "It's a sign you're supposed to get a dog!"

"Yes!" said Vicky. "That's why it showed up right before the dog did." She lowered her voice dramatically. "It's the promise of the rainbow."

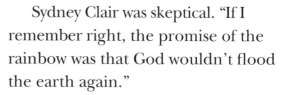

Sydney Clair was skeptical. "If I remember right, the promise of the rainbow was that God wouldn't flood the earth again."

"Sure, the promise to *Noah*. But maybe the promise to *you* is something different!" said Ann.

"Like a dog, of course!" said Vicky.

Sydney Clair chewed her bottom lip while she studied the rainbow. She doubted God would send her a sign like that. She went to church with her parents, but she didn't know God like her parents seemed to. They talked to God like he was a friend. Still, she really liked the idea of the rainbow being from God. Maybe . . . maybe it was possible. Vicky was right that it showed up just before the dog bounded into the picture. "Maybe you two are on to something." Sydney Clair smiled as she thought about owning Trouble. She could at least ask Mother and Dad to let her have him. "Let's go talk to my parents!"

Sydney Clair looked at Mother's new electric mixer sitting on the counter. She remembered how Mother had hinted to Dad how much she wanted it for Christmas last year. Would Mother remember what it was like to really, really want something?

"Twenty-five dollars is a lot of money," Mother murmured as she cut out paper shapes at the kitchen table. Her part-time job at the library included decorating the bulletin boards. "Does this look like France?" she asked.

"A dog is a lot of responsibility," said Dad.

"I promise to take care of him. I will! Please!" said Sydney Clair.

Across the room, Ann and Vicky nodded their heads.

Dad sat down at the table and turned to Mother. "I had a dog when I was growing up," he said.

Mother looked up from her project. "But the money. . . . "

"I'll raise it myself," blurted out Sydney Clair.

"Twenty-five dollars?" asked Dad. "What are you going to do? Get a job?"

"If I need to. I could do it!"

"Trust me. It's not that easy." Dad cast a sideways glance at Mother.

"We'll help. Right, Vicky?" said Ann.

"Right!" Vicky agreed.

"Well, how can we turn that down?" asked Dad.

Mother held up her shapes. "Don't count on me to help. I've got my hands full trying to keep my job at the library."

Penny, Sydney Clair's teenage sister, came in from the living room, where she'd been watching *Gilligan's Island.*

She was wearing her white vinyl go-go boots, as usual. She'd hardly taken them off since she'd bought them two months ago. "What's going on at the library, Mother?"

"My supervisor, Mrs. Witt, is considering hiring a full-time person."

"Far out," said Penny. "A full-time job."

"I don't want to work full-time," said Mother. "But I also don't want to leave. I enjoy working part-time, and I'm trying to help Mrs. Witt see how good I am." She held up a shape.

"Italy," said Sydney Clair.

"Why *not* work full-time?" said Penny. "Women have a right to work and find happiness and satisfaction outside the home."

Sydney Clair shifted from one foot to the other. She wanted to steer the conversation back to getting a dog, but she knew it would be rude to interrupt.

"Women also have the right to be at home if they choose," said Dad. "And happiness is a gift from God, not something that comes from being more like men."

Penny rolled her eyes. "Well, it sounds square to stay at home all day." She grabbed a cookie off the table and went back to the living room to see the end of her show.

"So, may I?" asked Sydney Clair. "May I get Trouble?"

Mother and Dad exchanged glances.

Dad took a deep breath. "If you earn the money yourself and take care of the dog . . . feed him, walk him, bathe him—"

Sydney Clair squealed, and so did Ann and Vicky. Sydney Clair couldn't believe it! Trouble was going to be her very own dog!

♡ ♡ ♡

"So how are we going to raise twenty-five dollars?" asked Sydney Clair the next day, sitting inside her playhouse with Ann and Vicky. Dad had put the roof on last week and promised he'd get to the doors and windows before the summer was over.

"We could baby-sit," suggested Vicky.

"I don't think we're old enough," said Sydney Clair. She didn't know any parents in the neighborhood who'd let ten-year-olds watch their children.

"We could sell cookies," said Ann.

"Or put on a play and charge admission," said Vicky.

"Or clean houses," said Sydney Clair.

"Or paint houses."

"Or paint works of art and sell them."

"Or cut hair."

None of the ideas seemed quite right. Suddenly Ann stuck her finger high in the air and shouted, "I've got it! A dog wash!"

"It's perfect. It's so hot all the dogs will want baths," said Sydney Clair.

"I don't know," said Vicky. "Don't you think we'll get dirty doing that?"

Sydney Clair exchanged looks with Ann. Vicky could be a bit prissy at times.

"Of course not," said Ann.

"We'll make sure you don't get dirty," said Sydney Clair.

"Well. . . . " Vicky hesitated. "Okay then."

Ann jumped out of her seat. "Hot dog! Let's get started!"

Sydney Clair clapped her hands. She had the best friends in the whole world! *And pretty soon I'm going to have a dog too!* she thought.

CHAPTER 2

Dog Wash

"Okay, we've got a laundry bucket, hose, bubble bath, cleaning rags and sponges, and a cool sign." Sydney Clair looked at the booth in her front yard, set up with a sign that read DOG WASH 25 CENTS. "I think we're ready for our grand opening!"

It didn't take long for a line of schnauzers, poodles, and basset hounds to form. Everyone out walking a dog that day seemed to think a dog washing was a good idea. Some of the dog owners started complaining about the wait.

"Tell them to leave their dogs here and come back in half an hour," Sydney Clair said to Ann. She took a break from sudsing down a squirmy Labrador puppy to oversee the situation. Twelve dogs were tied to the three trees in her front yard, some of them fighting, and all of them barking up a storm.

Across the street, Mrs. Blanchett shouted out her window, "Those dogs are making too much racket!"

Sydney Clair looked at Ann and Vicky, both elbow deep in suds. "Okay, time for a new plan," she said. "We need an assembly line. Ann, you entertain the dogs so they quiet down. I'll wash. Vicky, you dry."

"Groovy. That'll be the cleanest job," Vicky said. "I already noticed a spot on my dress."

 Ann found a hat to put on and started acting like a clown for the dogs, which quieted down some- what to watch the show.

Sydney Clair finished the poodle she was working on, handed the dog off to Vicky for drying, and called to Ann to bring the next dog.

"This one's going to be a challenge, I think," said Ann, lugging over the most massive Doberman pinscher that Sydney Clair had ever seen.

"I can handle it," said Sydney Clair. She noticed a name tag on the dog's collar.

"Okay, Buster," she said. "We're going to give you a little bath."

Next to her, Vicky was drying a poodle. "This dog's name is Francie. That's kind of pretty, don't you think, Sydney Clair?"

"It's okay for a girl dog."

"Are you going to give Trouble a new name?"

"Yes, but I have to think about it." Sydney Clair paused, loosening her grip on Buster. "It has to be a special name. Something with a lot of meaning." She poured more water over the Doberman and noticed him tighten every muscle in his huge body. "Don't be afraid," she told him.

But a look in his eye told her that it wasn't the water bothering him. She turned to see what he was looking at and gasped. Mrs. Blanchett's cat was peering out of the bushes on the other side of the lawn.

"Uh-oh."

She tightened her grip on Buster again, but two seconds too late. Buster bounded out of the water, dumping the bucket onto its side, and plowed over Vicky, knocking her to the ground. He raced across the front yard toward the poor cat, with Sydney Clair close behind.

"Buster! Buster! Come back!" she screamed.

The cat hissed and raced off in the opposite direction. Buster picked up speed.

The poodle squirmed away from Vicky and took off after Buster.

"Ann, help!" shouted Sydney Clair.

Ann stopped the clown act and took off toward the front corner of the lawn, to try to stop the runaway dogs. But Buster, with Francie still behind him, veered around her and came back past the dogs near the tree. One of the dogs Ann had been entertaining got loose and joined in the chase.

"Vicky! Get the dogs!" called Sydney Clair.

Vicky was still lying on the ground after being trampled by Buster. "My dress!" she shouted, noticing a big tear and muddy footprints all over her lavender shift.

Sydney Clair saw the animals bounding toward her

mother's garden. Sydney Clair lunged at Francie, the nearest loose dog, who was digging up one of the rosebushes. The dogs still tied to the trees yelped as though cheering on their favorite contender.

A white Corvair convertible with the top down pulled into Sydney Clair's driveway.

"What is going on here?" shouted Vicky's mother as she got out of the car.

Sydney Clair, yanking Francie out of the flower bed, remembered how protective Mrs. Parker was about her sporty new car.

"I said, What is going on here?" Mrs. Parker stomped across the yard to look at Vicky's tattered dress. Her high heels dug into the soft lawn.

Francie, wet and muddy, wriggled out of Sydney Clair's arms and ran for the still-open door of the car.

"Mrs. Parker, your car door!" Sydney Clair shouted. It was too late. The drippy, dirty poodle hopped into the car.

"Get that thing out of there!" Mrs. Parker screamed.

Mrs. Blanchett's cat had escaped up a tree in a neighboring yard. Ann wrestled Buster to the ground and dragged him back to the front of the yard while Sydney Clair collected Francie and the other dogs. Vicky helped tie the dogs to the tree. Then Sydney Clair turned to face Vicky's mother. "We're sorry, ma'am. We were just trying to make money," Sydney Clair explained.

"Well, Vicky's dress is ruined . . . and my new seats are covered in mud!"

"We're sorry, ma'am," Sydney Clair repeated.

"I'll clean your car," Ann offered. She picked up the overturned bucket and searched for a sponge.

"Nonsense. I'll get it cleaned myself. This is ridiculous. You should be proper young ladies, not chasing after muddy dogs. Vicky will not be a part of any of this. Get into the back seat, young lady." She shook her finger at Vicky.

"Yes, Mother," said Vicky. She cast an apologetic glance at Ann and Sydney Clair before crawling inside the convertible.

"Whose idea was this? Washing dogs! Young ladies in my day would think of no such thing. They would be knitting or gardening. Dog washing, indeed!" Mrs. Parker was still lecturing as she brushed off the driver's seat, slammed her door shut, and drove away.

Vicky waved to her friends as the car raced off.

Sydney Clair and Ann looked at the dogs and back at each other.

"We really are a mess," said Ann, a giggle in her voice.

Sydney Clair started laughing too. "You have a paw print on your forehead."

"I don't think we should do this again," said Ann.

"I think you're right. I've had enough dog washing. "Let's finish up the dogs we have and call it a day."

Sydney Clair turned the bucket right side up and stuck the hose in it. "But I still need money. I still want to get a dog."

"You still want a dog after this whole mess?" asked Ann.

"Of course. I'm going to have a well-behaved dog."

"Promise?" asked Ann.

"Promise," said Sydney Clair. "My dog will never do anything like this."

"*The Ed Sullivan Show* has never been as righteous as when the Beatles were on," said Penny. She had big pink rollers in her hair. The Wilcox family always watched the Sunday-evening show together.

Mr. Wilcox chuckled. "Well, it's certainly quieter around here when they're not on."

"The Beatles are so bad," said Penny.

"I thought you liked them," said Dad.

"I do!"

"But you just said they are bad."

"The good kind of bad," Penny said. "They're boss!"

"And that's good?"

"Yeah, you know, *bad* is good, and *righteous* is a gas."

Dad shook his head. "I feel like we're talking two different languages."

The credits rolled across the screen, and Dad reached over Penny, who was lounging on the floor, to turn the television off. Mother stood up from the couch. "I'd better go make sure I have money set out for the milkman tomorrow morning."

"I'm going out to the playhouse," said Sydney Clair.

Mother raised her eyebrows. "It's nearly dark."

"I won't be out long. May I?"

"Fifteen minutes," Mother agreed. "Then you need to get ready for bed."

Sydney Clair saw lightning bugs flashing across the lawn as she walked outside. She sat on the scratchy lawn chair inside her playhouse and peered through the framed window opening. Thousands of stars glittered in the night sky. It was stunning.

Dad's head peeked in the open window. "Admiring the moon?" he asked.

"Yes," she said. "Thank you again for my playhouse."

"I'll have it done soon enough." He looked up. "The stars are beautiful. God sure gave us an amazing world."

"It makes me want to be an astronaut," said Sydney Clair.

"I can imagine the *Gemini 4* crew had a pretty incredible view of the world from up there," Dad said.

"Do you think people will ever walk on the moon?" asked Sydney Clair.

"I think that's what they're working toward. Maybe when you're an astronaut."

"I'd be too afraid of the moon beings," she said.

"Maybe they'll send dogs up first to check it out," said Dad. The Russians started the space travel race by sending up dogs in rocket ships.

"Maybe instead of me, my dog will go to the moon," said Sydney Clair. She pictured her golden retriever looking out a rocket window while chewing on a dog biscuit.

"You'll have to train him to wear a fishbowl on his head," Dad said, chuckling.

Sydney Clair laughed. Then she grew quiet, watching the sky. "Why do you think God made the world?" she asked.

"I think he wanted someone to love, so he created us. And because he loves us, he gave us a beautiful world to live in."

"Do you think he wants us to be happy?"

"Indeed. We have his Word on it. The Bible says, Jesus came that we might have life 'abundantly.' *Abundantly* means really happy."

Sydney Clair thought about that. She'd never considered that God had created the stars and the moon and the trees and the clouds and rainbows for her—so *she* would be happy. And if he gave her the rainbow, maybe it did mean she was supposed to get a dog—just like Ann and Vicky thought!

Cold, Refreshing
Lemonade
5¢

Chapter 3

Sour or Sweet

The next morning, Sydney Clair sat with Ann out on the sidewalk.

Ann wiped some sweat off her forehead. "How much money did we make Saturday?"

"Three dollars," said Sydney Clair. "But I had to give money to Mrs. Parker to have her car cleaned, and I had to pay Mother for the rosebush the poodle ruined, so I'm down to zero again."

Ann sighed. "Do we have to raise money again today? Can't we just go to the park? Or, better yet, go to the pool for a swim?"

Sydney Clair was tempted. She knew a lot of their friends would be at the community pool. Doing a cannonball into the water would feel really good right now, but she was determined. She wanted this dog more than anything.

"We'll come up with a better idea this time," said Sydney Clair.

"But Vicky's not even here to help us," moaned Ann. "Do you think she'll show up?"

As if on cue, Vicky turned the corner on her bike.

"My mother almost didn't let me come over today," she said. "She told me I could play as long as I promised to stay clean." She got off her bike and wiped imaginary dirt off her blue pedal pushers.

Sydney Clair was glad to see Vicky. It always felt strange when one of the three was missing, and they were always there for each other when one of them needed help. Sydney Clair and Ann had put together games and skits for Vicky when she broke her leg. And Vicky and Sydney Clair had cried with Ann when her grandmother died last year. Now all three of them needed to work together to get a dog for Sydney Clair.

"We have to think," said Sydney Clair. "There has to be a way we can make money."

"I'm sure there is," said Ann. "But I break out in a sweat every time I start thinking. I can't do anything until I get some lemonade or something."

"Yes," agreed Vicky. "Lemonade sounds so good."

Sydney Clair snapped her fingers. *Of course!* "That's it! A lemonade stand!"

Ann fumbled through the Wilcoxes' kitchen cabinets. "I don't even know how to make lemonade," she said. "My mother always makes it."

"It's not hard. I've made it plenty of times," said Sydney Clair. "A lemonade stand will be a big hit on the block. I know it!" She'd have enough money for her dog in no time.

"I'd better not spill anything on myself," said Vicky.

"Here, put these on." Sydney Clair handed Vicky and Ann aprons and put on one herself.

Ann slipped it over her neck. "Groovy! We look professional. Like real chefs."

Vicky pointed to the shelf above the hook where the aprons hung. "Is that a chef's hat up there?"

"Yes," Sydney Clair said. "Mother bought it for Dad when he tried to make a cake." She grinned. "It didn't help him cook any better though. The cake ended up raw in the middle and burnt on top."

"Would your parents mind if I wore it?" asked Ann.

"They won't care," Sydney Clair said. "Anyway, it will make us look like we are serving gourmet lemonade."

Sydney Clair started filling up Mother's largest jug with water. "I'll add the lemonade mix to this. You go to the pantry and get two cups of sugar. And, Vicky, could you get some ice from the trays in the freezer?"

"Where's the sugar?" called Ann from the pantry.

"Top shelf on the left," Sydney Clair called back. She smiled. This was going to be a whole lot easier than dog washing. She tried to calculate how many cups she'd have to sell at five cents each to make twenty-five dollars. *A whole lot* was the answer she came up with.

Sydney Clair held the pitcher while Ann poured in the sugar and Vicky added the ice. Then she stirred up the mixture. The lemony color looked perfectly refreshing.

"Now it's time to sample the merchandise," said Ann, reaching for the pitcher to pour herself a cup.

"No way," said Sydney Clair. "We need to sell as much as we can. Which means *we* can't have any." She grabbed the cup away from Ann and filled it up with water from the sink before handing it back.

"This is becoming less and less fun," Ann muttered.

"Now all we need to do is make some signs," said Sydney Clair.

♡ ♡ ♡

Sydney Clair found an old table in the garage to set up in the front yard under a tree. She covered it with one of Mother's red-and-white-checkered tablecloths. Vicky made a sign that said COLD, REFRESHING LEMONADE—5¢.

"I think our first two customers are coming," said Ann.

"It's Tommy Henderson," said Vicky. "He's *sooo* groovy."

Ann rolled her eyes at Sydney Clair.

"And I think Larry Warbler is with him," said Sydney Clair.

Tommy and Larry were showing off on their bikes, riding with no hands and their arms crossed. The boys stopped in front of the lemonade table. Their hair looked damp.

"Were you at the pool?" asked Vicky.

"Along with everyone else," said Larry. "Tommy did a back flip with a twist off the diving board. Nearly killed himself. The lifeguard made him get out. You should have been there."

"We have more important things to do," said Ann. "We need to earn money so Sydney Clair can get a dog."

Larry looked at the sign. "So you're selling lemonade?"

"That sounds really good right now," said Tommy. "Let's get some and take it to our secret clubhouse."

Sydney Clair tried not to smirk. Tommy Henderson would do anything for attention. But how they could call that tree house in his backyard a secret clubhouse was beyond her. Anyone walking alongside the house could see the **TOP SECRET. NO GIRLZ ALLOWED** sign clear as day. Sydney Clair was certain all they did was sit up there and read comic books or, occasionally, fight off imaginary space aliens.

Larry dug into his pocket for two nickels while Ann poured the lemonade.

"You carry the drinks, Larry," Tommy said.

"How can I climb up the ladder with the drinks?"

"Shhh. Don't talk about the ladder. Remember it's a secret."

The boys rode away, Tommy with his arms folded like an Indian chief and Larry balancing two cups of lemonade in his hands.

"They are such showoffs," Ann muttered.

"Well, we made our first sale," said Sydney Clair. The two coins made a satisfying *clang* as they hit the bottom of the money box.

Ann looked down the street. "Is that your dad?"

Sydney Clair looked up to see Dad in his Plymouth station wagon, motoring toward them. He pulled into the driveway, got out, and wiped his brow.

"What are you doing home so early?" asked Sydney Clair. The cement factory where Dad worked was about an hour away, and he usually didn't get home until after six.

"Cement dries too quickly in this heat," Dad said. "We rescheduled some of our jobs for tomorrow morning." He grinned over at the girls. "A lemonade stand! Now that's a great idea. I could really go for some."

Ann poured him a cupful.

"Five cents please, Mr. Wilcox," said Vicky, holding out an open palm.

Dad dropped in a nickel and took a long drink of lemonade. Suddenly he grimaced, spewed the drink out onto the sidewalk, and started coughing.

"What's wrong?" asked Ann.

"Is it too tart?" asked Vicky.

Sydney Clair poured herself a glass and took a sip. *Ugh!* It was awful!

Dad was still coughing. "I'm sorry, girls. It's . . . it's . . . what did you put in there?"

"Just sugar, lemonade mix, and water," said Sydney Clair. She was thoroughly confused.

"I don't think that's sugar," Dad said, shaking his head. "I'm going to go in and get some water. You should probably follow me and remake that lemonade."

"I put in two cups—just like Sydney Clair told me," said Ann.

Sydney Clair remembered that Mother kept an orange canister next to the glass sugar bowl.

"Did you take it out of the glass bowl?" asked Sydney Clair.

 "No, there wasn't much left. So I got it out of the orange canister."

Sydney Clair covered her face with her hands. "That wasn't sugar—that was salt!"

♡ ♡ ♡

"All right, let's try again," said Sydney Clair. This time she measured out the sugar.

"It *is* a little funny," said Vicky. "Think of the surprised look on Tommy's and Larry's faces when they try their lemonade."

Ann smiled. "Now I would pay five cents just to see that!"

Vicky watched as Sydney Clair carefully stirred the freshly mixed lemonade. "Maybe I could do gymnastics on the front lawn to draw a crowd," Vicky said. "Or I could sing! I know all the songs from *The Sound of Music*!"

Sydney Clair had seen that movie with her family at the drive-in theater. It was already one of her favorites. She'd even named her new doll Liesl, after one of the main characters.

Vicky started belting out her own rendition of "The Hills Are Alive"—severely off-key.

"Whoa, you'd better stop," Ann interrupted her. "We're trying to draw customers in, not scare them away."

Sydney Clair led the way back out to the front yard. Ann put the sign back in the ground and looked up the street to see if anyone was heading in their direction.

"Mrs. Patterson is out walking her dog. And I think that's Mr. Burton's car coming this way, and—uh-oh."

Sydney Clair stopped setting out cups and looked at Ann. "What is it?"

"We've got problems."

Chapter 4

Trouble

"Look." Ann pointed at the sign Larry held as he rode by on his bike.

LEMONADE FOR SALE. BEST LEMONADE ON THE BLOCK.

He turned the sign around. It read: **WILCOX LEMONADE STINKS!**

Sydney Clair looked up the street and there, standing behind a table of cups and a pitcher, stood Tommy Henderson. She fumed. "They're trying to put us out of business!"

Sydney Clair watched Mrs. Patterson stop at the boys' stand and buy a cup. She looked down at their own cups, lined up neatly side by side.

"No one's going to come down here now," said Ann.

"We can't give up," said Sydney Clair. "We just made a new batch. A good batch!"

Vicky looked doubtful. "They don't know that, though. And now they're telling everyone how horrible it was."

The line at the boys' lemonade stand was growing. "We have to do something." Sydney Clair thought for a minute.

"I think Mother made cookies this morning."

"Your mother makes the best cookies," said Ann.

"So we could add them to the menu. Everyone likes cookies!"

Vicky nodded. "That just might work."

Mother agreed to donate a plate of her snickerdoodle cookies.

"Are you sure you don't want *me* to make you a batch?" Dad teased. "I'd love to be zee gourmet chef for zee lemon-ade stand!"

"Thanks, Dad, but we've already had one disaster today," said Sydney Clair. "We don't need another."

Vicky and Ann giggled. But Sydney Clair hurried to load up a plate with cookies. She had a mission, and there was no time for lollygagging. "Come on, you two," she said.

Ann took the first turn riding her bike past the boys' lemonade stand, holding up the girls' new sign. **NEW IMPROVED LEMONADE! AND FRESH COOKIES! ONLY AT THE WILCOX REFRESHMENT STAND!** Surrounding the words were brightly painted yellow lemons.

Settled behind the table with Vicky, Sydney Clair smiled at people's interest in the sign. Mrs. Patterson and Mrs. Smith, who'd been walking together, looked down the street and headed toward the girls' stand. This was working! Customers were coming! A man walking a Scottish terrier that they'd washed the other day was coming from the opposite direction. And Mrs. Blanchett pulled into her driveway across the street. She waved to Sydney Clair.

"Cookies and lemonade sound wonderful! I'll be right over."
Sydney Clair was happy Mrs. Blanchett seemed to be over her
bad mood about the loud dogs and her poor panicked cat.

"We're getting all sorts of customers," said Vicky. "This
is great!"

Ann rode back past the girls. "How's it going?" she called.

"Terrific! You're doing swell!" shouted
Sydney Clair.

"Woo-hoo!" Ann started riding in
circles in the street in front of the stand.
"Hey, look! I'm Tommy Henderson." She
stuck the sign in the basket of her bike and
crossed her arms across her chest. "No hands!"

Sydney Clair did not have a good feeling about this.

Ann started riding faster, making a big circle. Then she
put her feet up on the handlebars.

"Look, no hands or feet!" Ann crowed. She waved her
arms over her head.

"Watch out for the curb!" shouted Vicky.

Ann's circle was too big. Her front tire jolted against the
curb, knocking Ann onto the ground and sending the bike
up over the sidewalk. Vicky dove right and Sydney Clair dove
left as the bike crashed into the table. Cookies, cups, and
lemonade flew into the air.

Sydney Clair rushed over to Ann. "Are you okay?"

"Yes," said Ann. She got up and brushed herself off and
then noticed the table. "Oh no!"

Sydney Clair followed her eyes. The lemonade pitcher
lay on the grass, empty. Cookies mingled with pieces of the
broken plate on the sidewalk, and plastic cups rolled into
the street.

Sydney Clair looked up toward Tommy's house. The boys were laughing. Mrs. Patterson and Mrs. Smith had turned around and were heading back to the boys' lemonade stand. The man with the Scottish terrier crossed the street, and Mrs. Blanchett stood in her driveway, shaking her head.

The Wilcox Lemonade Stand was out of business.

With a heavy sigh, Sydney Clair looked at her friends. "Are you sure that rainbow was a sign God wants me to have a dog?"

No one said a word.

Sydney Clair sat at the kitchen table with Ann and Vicky and Mother. "You can't give up," said Mother. She was cutting out more shapes for the library bulletin board.

"It sure seems pretty hopeless right now," Sydney Clair said. Ann and Vicky nodded. "I don't want to give up, but it seems like everything is going wrong."

Dad came into the kitchen. "I'm sorry things didn't work out like you hoped. I know you've tried very hard."

"Maybe we could put on a circus," suggested Vicky. "My cat can do somersaults. And I could probably get my little brother to swallow fire or something. . . . "

"Yes," Ann said. "And I could do my bicycle trick!"

"Hold on, hold on," Dad said. "Before you start having people swallow fire in our front yard, maybe we should look at a different route to getting you a dog."

He looked at Mother, who was watching him over her orange cutout of Mexico.

She nodded slowly. "Your dad and I have talked it over, and even though I'm still a little skeptical, I think he's right."

"What, what?" asked Sydney Clair. *What was Mother saying?*

Dad grinned. "How about if we were to give you a gift?"

"You'll *hire* us a fire swallower?" asked Vicky, her mouth open in awe.

"No, silly!" Ann hopped up and down. "He's going to get Sydney Clair her dog. Right, Mr. Wilcox?"

"That's the plan," said Dad. "How's that sound, Sydney Clair?"

Suddenly Dad's words registered. Sydney Clair realized she was standing there with her mouth open. She never expected this! How could Mother and Dad love her so much? She didn't know what else to do but erupt in squeals and jump up to give Dad and Mother the biggest hugs she could. "Yes, yes! Thank you!"

"Can we go with you to get Trouble?" asked Vicky.

"I don't see why not. Go ask your parents. We'll leave in a few minutes," Dad said.

Mother looked at Sydney Clair. "Remember now, gifts do come with responsibilities."

"Oh, I'll take such good care of Trouble! I promise. I'll feed him and brush him and wash him—"

"But just *him*, right?" asked Dad with a smile. "Don't invite the rest of the dogs in the neighborhood over for a bath too."

Sydney Clair kept grinning. "You can be sure of that!"

Morgan's Dog Breeding was nestled amid overgrown grass with two large, empty dog runs in the front yard. As Sydney Clair waited for Mr. Morgan to answer the door, she worried. What if someone else had already bought Trouble?

Finally Mr. Morgan opened the door, and Trouble galloped up behind him. Sydney Clair relaxed.

Mr. Morgan closed the door partway, just in time to keep Trouble inside. "May I help you?" he asked.

Dad responded heartily. "You sure can. I understand you have a dog for sale."

"Oh yes," Mr. Morgan continued. He didn't seem to recognize Sydney Clair. "We have several that were born about six weeks ago. Great show dogs. You'll have wonderful success with them in the arena. Award winners, all of them."

Sydney Clair waited for Mr. Morgan to take a breath. "We don't want those. We want that one." She pointed toward Trouble, his snout protruding from behind the door.

"The grown one?" Mr. Morgan peered at Sydney Clair more closely, then at Ann and Vicky standing beside her. "Well, I'll be! You're the little girls I talked to the other day."

Sydney Clair nodded. She didn't like being referred to as a little girl, but right now all she wanted was her dog.

Mr. Morgan opened the door, keeping hold of Trouble's collar. "I'd pretty much given up on getting rid of this one. But he sure seems to like you."

The dog broke free from Mr. Morgan and drenched Sydney Clair in wet doggy kisses. She loved every lick. Finally, a dog of her own!

Dad opened his wallet. "I believe twenty-five dollars is the price?"

Mr. Morgan nodded. He handed Dad a leash and clipped one end to Trouble's collar. Dad handed the leash to Sydney Clair, and the entire crew plus a very excited dog piled back into the Plymouth station wagon. Sydney Clair scratched Trouble behind the ears. She felt giddy. *I'm not down in the dumps anymore,* she thought. She was sure she'd never be unhappy again.

On the living room floor after dinner, waiting for the family's devotional time to begin, Sydney Clair didn't even

care about the doggy drool as she nuzzled her face into Trouble's neck.

"I need to think of a new name for him," she said. "He's not trouble at all."

"How about Drooler?" suggested Penny. "He sure seems to do *that* well."

"No," said Sydney Clair. "I need to think of the perfect name. The name that really fits him."

Dad leaned over Trouble. "Now, if you're going to be part of the family, you'll need to pay attention as we talk about God. No slobbering on the Bible," he joked.

Trouble looked up as if he understood.

"Where's your mother?" asked Dad.

"She's on the phone," said Penny, taking her seat on the floor beside Sydney Clair.

When Mother sat down, she looked worried. "That was Mrs. Witt. She wants me to come in tomorrow. She has something she wants to talk over with me." Mother sighed.

Dad nodded. "Well, let's get started then. I think we were in Matthew 7."

Sydney Clair was soon distracted. The dog rolled on his back and begged her with his eyes to give him a good tummy scratch. She was more than happy to oblige. Mother and Dad said the Bible was one way God talks to us, but that didn't make sense to Sydney Clair. Why would God talk to them when there were millions of people on the planet? She pictured God far, far away—barely aware of the ant-like people wandering around on earth.

Then she heard Dad reading words that got her attention.

"Ask, and it shall be given you; seek, and ye shall find; knock, and it shall be opened unto you: For every one that asketh receiveth; and he that seeketh findeth; and to him that knocketh it shall be opened. Or what man is there of you, whom if his son ask bread, will he give him a stone? Or if he ask a fish, will he give him a serpent? If ye then, being evil, know how to give good gifts unto your children, how much more shall your Father which is in heaven give good things to them that ask him?"

Sydney Clair scratched Trouble's ears. He definitely was a good gift. But how could her parents be evil?

"Was there a verse in there that means you and Mother are evil?" she asked when Dad had finished reading.

Dad chuckled. "What that verse is saying is that even though parents like us, who aren't perfect and who mess up, want to give you girls good gifts, think of how much more God, who *is* perfect, wants to give."

"You and Mother got me the best gift ever, though." Sydney Clair patted Trouble.

"You know, I think Trouble is a great example of how God gives us gifts," Mother said. "You never did earn enough money to buy a dog, but your dad and I got him for you anyway. That is called *grace*."

"Grace?" Sydney Clair was confused. She had only heard that word as Vicky's middle name.

"Grace is being given something we can't earn. God gave us grace through his Son, Jesus. That's the gift that keeps giving."

Penny looked distracted. "May I be excused now? I told Margo I'd call her. We're going to meet a friend of hers at Frankie's Porch for sodas."

"In a minute," Dad said. "After we pray."

Trouble lifted his head and nudged Sydney Clair's hand. He wasn't done being scratched yet.

Dad led them in prayer. "Father God, thank you for how much you love us and the good gifts you give us in your Son, Jesus Christ. We love you. Amen."

"Amen," echoed Penny. "Now may I call Margo?"

"You may," said Dad. "Who are you meeting?"

"Margo's cousin. She's involved in some group at college called Campus Crusade. She wants to talk to us about it. And afterward we're going cruising with Hank and David."

Mother reminded them all that cookies and milk were in the kitchen. "We still have some snickerdoodles left. And we can talk about our vacation."

"I don't know if we have the budget to get away on vacation right now," Mother continued at the kitchen table. "Maybe in a few months." She paused. "Unless you want to start looking for another job, Wade. One that pays what you're worth."

Dad shrugged noncommittally.

Penny came into the kitchen and grabbed a cookie. "If you took that full-time job at the library, we'd have extra money, Mother," she said.

"Still not interested," Mother said.

Penny blew an upward puff of air, splaying her bangs. "Mother, you really need to think about what you're doing to support equality among women. Womankind is counting on you."

"I think womankind is doing fine," Mother said with a smile.

"What are you talking about?" asked Sydney Clair.

Penny sighed dramatically. "It's about making sure women don't get stepped on by men who want to limit our potential and keep us at home." She peered out the kitchen window. "Margo's going to be here any minute. I've got to finish getting ready. ."

Sydney Clair saw Mother and Dad exchange glances.

Dad leaned forward. "There are women who are fighting to guarantee all women have equal rights with men. It's a good idea in some aspects, but some women want to take it to the extreme. They want to be treated just like men in everything."

"So are you fighting with these women, Mother?" asked Sydney Clair.

"Well," said Mother, "I definitely don't want my daughters being drafted and sent to war." Sydney Clair had heard about the Vietnam War happening on the other side of the world, but she didn't understand what the fighting was about.

Suddenly a scream rose from another room.

"*Nooooo!*" Penny wailed. "Not my boots!"

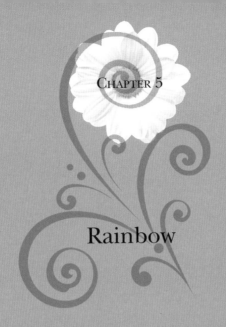

Chapter 5

Rainbow

Penny stormed into the kitchen, a look of horror on her face. She held up one of her go-go boots. "Look at what Trouble did!" She plopped it on the table so everyone could see the chewed-up heel. "You were wrong, Sydney Clair. His name fits him perfectly."

"Where is Trouble now?" Dad asked.

"He'd better not be in our room," Penny said to Sydney Clair.

Sydney Clair ran to the bedroom she shared with her sister. "My doll! Where is my doll?" She always left Liesl propped up in the middle of her bed. But Liesl was gone!

Sydney Clair scurried through the house along with Penny, Mother, and Dad, calling, "Trouble, Trouble! Where are you?"

"I found your doll, Sydney Clair!" Penny hollered from Mother and Dad's bedroom. "That is . . . what's left of her."

Sydney Clair ran into her parents' room. She shrieked at the sight of Liesl—one arm was covered with teeth marks, and the other arm was gone completely.

"I'm sorry, darling," said Mother. "I know Liesl is your favorite. Maybe if we find the arm, we can sew it back on."

Dad came in the bedroom. "Well, I found Trouble, cowering in the bathroom. He knew he was in trouble, I guess. I chained him up outside."

Mother smiled. "I'm glad we stopped his reign of terror."

"Not soon enough, I'm afraid," said Dad.

Sydney Clair followed Dad, Penny, and Mother to the living room. She gasped. All the cutouts Mother had spent hours creating for the library bulletin boards lay scattered around the room, as if the world had exploded. Some were chewed beyond recognition, but most were torn and wet with slobber. Sydney Clair couldn't see a single one that was still usable.

"I've been working on this all week," said Mother, her voice barely above a whisper. Without another word, she began picking up the cutouts and throwing them in the wastebasket.

Sydney Clair started to help.

"Sydney Clair," Mother said, without looking at her. "I think you should go out and discipline your dog. And then you need to go to bed."

Mother must wonder why we got Trouble, thought Sydney Clair. Was Mother angry at *her* for ruining the bulletin board project? Trouble was her dog, after all. The dog she'd wanted more than anything.

Sydney Clair rushed outside and slumped down next to Trouble. "You were a bad dog," she said. "I don't know how you could do that. We were only in the kitchen for ten minutes."

Trouble tilted his head and perked up his ears.

"And you ruined my Liesl doll and Penny's boot."

Trouble laid his head between his paws.

Sydney Clair scratched behind his ears. "You have to learn. You just have to learn."

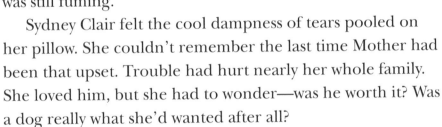

When she went to bed, Sydney Clair lay under the covers, hugging her pillow instead of Liesl. She pretended to be asleep when Penny came in. She heard Penny throw her loafers in the closet—the plain brown loafers she hadn't worn since getting her beloved boots. Penny was still fuming.

Sydney Clair felt the cool dampness of tears pooled on her pillow. She couldn't remember the last time Mother had been that upset. Trouble had hurt nearly her whole family. She loved him, but she had to wonder—was he worth it? Was a dog really what she'd wanted after all?

The following morning Sydney Clair sat quietly in the seat next to Mother as they drove to the library.

"While I meet with Mrs. Witt, I want you to find a book on dog training," Mother said.

Sydney Clair nodded.

Mother reached for her hand. "Did I tell you we are having chicken and dumplings for dinner?"

Sydney Clair had to smile. She knew Mother wasn't angry any more. But making her favorite, chicken and dumplings, wasn't necessary. After all, her dog did ruin Mother's plan for proving her value as a part-time employee.

The library fascinated Sydney Clair. How could a room with so many people be so quiet? She found the shelf with the dog-training titles and chose one called *Training Man's Best Friend.*

Mrs. Witt was at the front desk. "Hello, Sydney Clair," she said as she stamped the card in the front pocket of the book Sydney Clair was checking out.

"Hello, Mrs. Witt."

"I just finished talking with your mother."

Sydney Clair nodded. She wondered if Mrs. Witt had fired her mother, but she dared not ask. And she didn't see Mother anywhere around.

Mrs. Witt peered over her horn-rimmed glasses. "She said you've acquired a new pet."

"Yes, ma'am."

"I understand he's going to take a little work."

"Yes, ma'am," Sydney Clair said again.

Mrs. Witt removed her glasses and let them hang on the chain around her neck. "There's something special about a girl and her pet. My grandfather got me a cat when I was about your age. I wanted a fluffy white cat more than anything."

A cat wouldn't chew up dolls, thought Sydney Clair.

"Grandfather died later that year," Mrs. Witt continued, "and when I think of him, I always remember the day he gave me that cat." She had a faraway look in her eyes.

Sydney Clair shifted from one foot to the other. She didn't want to interrupt Mrs. Witt, but she wanted to go find her mother and see what happened.

Mrs. Witt put on her glasses again and smiled. "Just remember to appreciate the giver as well as the gift," she said. "Here's your book."

Sydney Clair walked toward the front doors of the library to wait for Mother. She appreciated her parents for getting Trouble for her. She loved that they knew how much getting him meant to her. And if it came down to it, she decided, she'd give him up if that was best for the family. She just hoped that wasn't the case.

"Ready to go?" Mother asked. She seemed to be in a good mood.

Sydney Clair nodded. She linked arms with Mother, and they started down the steps together toward the car.

"Mother, do you and Dad regret getting me a dog?"

Mother smiled. "Actually, I think Trouble was a gift from your dad to you and a gift from God to me."

"What do you mean?"

"Your dad wanted to get you a dog because he loves you and he knew how much you wanted one. He saw how hard you tried to earn the money to buy Trouble." Mother took a deep breath. "And God gave *us* that dog because he knows my heart as well. When I was explaining to Mrs. Witt what happened with the cutouts, I suddenly came up with the idea of having a weekly children's reading and craft time, where children could do different crafts to decorate the bulletin boards. Mrs. Witt loved the idea! She wants me to coordinate the library's community activities, and that is only a part-time position!"

"If Trouble hadn't ruined my cutouts," Mother continued as they got into the car, "I wouldn't have needed to come up with another plan to decorate the bulletin boards. I never would have thought of a children's reading and craft time, and I never would have gotten this new part-time job!"

Sydney Clair was glad things worked out for her mother, but she still missed her poor Liesl doll, and Penny was still upset about her boot. "I'm glad at least one of the family is happy."

"You're not happy?" Mother asked. She didn't start the car.

Sydney Clair shook her head. "I love Trouble. I really do. But I thought getting him would change things. I thought somehow having a dog would keep me from being sad. But it didn't." She explained about the day in the front yard when she and her friends saw the rainbow. "But last night I felt more sad and lonely than I did even *before* I got Trouble."

Mother's eyes were filled with understanding. "Maybe the gift of the dog and the rainbow were signs of something much bigger. There is only one thing that will keep you from feeling discontentment in life, and it's not gifts, but the giver. And the giver is God."

The giver? Sydney Clair remembered what Mrs. Witt had said inside the library. *Appreciate the giver.* Come to think of it, that sounded a little bit like what Dad read in their devotional time the night before. "It's like that verse Dad read about how God wants to give us good things."

"That's right!" said Mother. "Your dad and I can give you a dog, but God can give you something so much better. He loves you even more than we do—and we love you an awful lot!"

Sydney Clair thought about what Dad said the night they watched the stars together. "Dad says God made such a beautiful world because he loves us. I never thought of God as loving me like that."

"But he does," Mother said. "He had you in mind before the earth was created. He loved you before you were born. He knows you better than your dad and I know you, even better than *you* know you." Mother cupped Sydney Clair's chin in her hand. "We were created to be in relationship with God and his Son, Jesus. That's what we were made for, and part of us is incomplete until we have it."

Sydney Clair listened intently. She remembered her empty feeling as she lay on the front lawn with her friends—that feeling that something was missing. When Trouble came along, she'd thought he was the answer.

Mother continued. "Sometimes we try to fill that space with God's gifts—the many good things he gives us. But they're never enough, and God knows that. The Bible says, 'For God so loved the world, that he gave his only begotten Son, that whosoever believeth in him should not perish, but have everlasting life.' Only God's best gift will satisfy us—the gift of his Son. The gift of a relationship with him."

Dad loved me and gave me Trouble. And God loves me even more! thought Sydney Clair. She didn't have to earn it. She just had to want it. Sydney Clair knew this is what she wanted —God's gift of grace: Jesus.

Mother slipped her hand in Sydney Clair's. "Do you remember the rest of what Dad read? The Bible says, 'Ask, and it shall be given you; seek, and ye shall find; knock, and it shall be opened unto you.'"

Sydney Clair held her breath.

"Would you like to invite Jesus to come live inside you?" Mother asked. "He won't come as a guest. You must surrender your heart to him."

Sydney Clair knew this was a big decision. But she also knew the answer. "Yes, I want to give God my heart."

Mother closed her eyes and prayed, "Dear God, thank you that you give us good gifts. Thank you for Jesus, your gift, who saves us and fills us with lasting gifts." She squeezed Sydney Clair's hand.

Sydney Clair took a deep breath and continued, "Dear God, would you let Jesus come live inside me?" She looked up at Mother, not knowing the right words to say.

Mother whispered, "Remember, he knows our hearts."

Sydney Clair smiled. She didn't have to say the right words. God knew that she wanted him to make her heart his home. And she knew he was already there.

♡ ♡ ♡

When Mother and Sydney Clair pulled into the driveway, Dad was on the front lawn with Trouble.

"Sit. Sit!" Dad said. Trouble seemed to be paying attention until a butterfly flitted past. He bounded after it.

Sydney Clair couldn't help but smile as she saw the sloppy grin plastered on the dog's face.

"We have some good news and some great news." Mother said.

"I could use some great news *and* a cool glass of lemonade," Dad said.

Sydney Clair and Mother followed Dad and Trouble into the house. As Trouble lapped up water from his bowl in the kitchen, Mother shared about her new part-time job at the library.

"Now for the great news. I'll let Sydney Clair share," Mother said.

Sydney Clair told Dad about the afternoon when she, Ann, and Vicky saw the rainbow—the day she first met Trouble. She told him about what Mrs. Witt had said, and how she realized God is the giver of good gifts and the best gift of all, Jesus. "So I prayed and asked Jesus to come live inside me," she finished with an excited grin.

Dad wrapped her in a giant bear hug. "I'm so proud of you," he said. "And so happy."

Sydney Clair squeezed back.

"And it all started with God sending you a rainbow," Mother said.

Suddenly Sydney Clair let go of Dad and clapped her hands. "I have a new name for Trouble!" she said. "Rainbow! And we'll call him Bo for short."

Mother and Dad looked at one another and smiled.

"I think that's the perfect name," Mother said.

And Sydney Clair knew it was too. She gave Bo a hug, and Bo gave her a big doggy kiss.

The Space Race

In the space race of the 1960s, the United States and the Soviet Union both wanted to claim superiority in space to increase their nation's security.

On May 5, 1961, when John F. Kennedy was president, Alan Shepard became the first American in space. Inside his tiny Mercury spacecraft, which he named *Freedom 7*, Shepard rode a Redstone booster on a fifteen-minute flight.

John Glenn became the first American to orbit the earth. On February 12, 1962, inside his *Friendship 7* spacecraft, Glenn circled the globe three times, marveling at the beauty of sunrises and sunsets and then sweating through a fiery reentry into Earth's atmosphere.

As important as these missions were for the U.S. space program, to many they were overshadowed by the Soviet flights. In 1963, a former cotton mill worker and parachute jumper named Valentina Tereshkova became the first woman in space, logging almost three days in space.

In the United States, the National Aeronautics and Space Administration (NASA) responded with Gemini, the most sophisticated spacecraft yet created. Gemini astronauts utilized an on-board computer that enabled them to change their orbit in flight—something no Soviet crew had yet accomplished. In just twenty short months, between March 1965 and November 1966, ten Gemini crews pioneered the techniques necessary for a lunar mission.

Finally, the United States' *Apollo 11*, commanded by Neil Armstrong and Buzz Aldrin, landed on the moon's surface on July 20, 1969. With millions watching him by satellite on their televisions, Neil Armstrong said, "That's one small step for man, one giant leap for mankind."

The Jesus Movement

The Jesus Movement during the 1960s in the United States was predominantly made up of young people of high school and college age. Many of these had been involved in either the civil rights protest activities of the 1960s or the drug-oriented "hippie" counterculture.

The hippies' quest led to misery, boredom, and loneliness. In contrast, the Jesus Movement offered a meaningful life, a reason for living. Many groups that were considered part of the Jesus Movement are still thriving today, including Campus Crusade for Christ, Fellowship of Christian Athletes, Youth for Christ International, and Young Life.

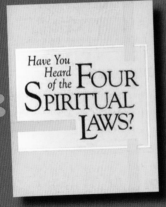

In 1965 Bill Bright and his wife, Vonette, founders of Campus Crusade for Christ, wrote *Have You Heard of the Four Spiritual Laws?* It is likely the most widely distributed religious booklet in history, with more than 2.5 billion copies printed to date. You can read the text of this evangelism tool at this website: http://www.campuscrusade.com/fourlawsflash.htm.

Small Screen: Television

Television became an essential item in many American households in the 1960s. TV prices began to come down, so most everyone could afford to buy a TV set. But people were not quite "couch potatoes" yet!

To sit in front of "the tube" for more than a couple of hours was considered lazy and lacking in intelligence. Being a TV addict was very much taboo! But TV shows were clean and were considered wholesome entertainment.

The Andy Griffith Show

First telecast: October 3, 1960 • Last telecast: September 16, 1968

The Andy Griffith Show humorously depicted life in Mayberry, a fictional North Carolina community. Andy Griffith played Sheriff Andy Taylor, with Ron Howard as his son, Opie, and Don Knotts as his clumsy cousin and deputy, Barney Fife.

The Dick Van Dyke Show

First telecast: October 3, 1961 • Last telecast: June 1, 1966

In this show, Dick Van Dyke played Robert "Rob" Petrie, the head comedy writer for a fictional New York TV variety show. Mary Tyler Moore played Rob's wife, Laura.

Gilligan's Island

First telecast: September 26, 1964 • Last telecast: September 4, 1967

Gilligan's Island featured the comic misadventures of seven shipwrecked castaways on a previously uninhabited island.

The Ed Sullivan Show

Running from 1948 to 1971, The Ed Sullivan Show *was the longest-running variety series in television history.*

In 1964, Ed Sullivan signed the Beatles for three landmark appearances. Their first slot, on February 9, 1964, came at the height of Beatlemania, the beginning of a revolution in music, fashion, and attitude. One of the most watched programs in the history of television, the episode gave Sullivan the biggest ratings of his career.

Big Screen: Movies

Many great movies made their debut on the big screen in the 1960s. Two favorites for the entire family both featured Julie Andrews in the leading role.

Mary Poppins

This 1964 musical, starring Julie Andrews and Dick Van Dyke, was based on a series of children's books written by P. L. Travers about a mysterious, magical English nanny, Mary Poppins.

The Sound of Music

In 1965 another movie musical, *The Sound of Music*, retold the memoir of Maria von Trapp. The movie was based on a book written by Howard Lindsay and Russel Crouse. With music by Richard Rodgers and lyrics by Oscar Hammerstein II, famous songs from the movie include "The Sound of Music (The Hills Are Alive)," "Edelweiss," "My Favorite Things," "Climb Ev'ry Mountain," and "Do-Re-Mi."

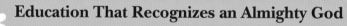
YE SHALL KNOW THE TRUTH AND THE TRUTH SHALL MAKE YOU FREE

Education That Recognizes an Almighty God
Many people, academic institutions, and government offices acknowledged the presence and leadership of almighty God, as testified by the biblical inscription on the landmark Tower on the University of Texas campus: "Ye shall know the truth, and the truth shall make you free" (John 8:32).

Girls 'n Grace COLLECTIONS

We celebrate the strength and wisdom that we have in Christ, so today and into the future we can become all that God has purposed.

Girls 'n Grace 18" dolls have been beautifully sculpted by the renowned doll artist Dianna Eff

International characters!

Discover an international community of Girls 'n Grace from Africa, the United Kingdom, India, Peru, and more!

I Can Through Christ!®

Girls 'n Grace Like Me! Collection

Choose a doll that looks like you!

Choose your Girls 'n Grace doll today!

Each 18" Girls 'n Grace doll comes with:

a doll-sized Bible with thirty-two verses on God's grace!

Secret Code!
a tag with a secret address code to an online virtual world —Girls 'n Grace Place!

a designer box to store your doll and her accessories.

Contemporary historical characters from the 1960s to the 1990s!

I Can Through Christ!®

Sydney Clair
1960s

Patrice
1960s

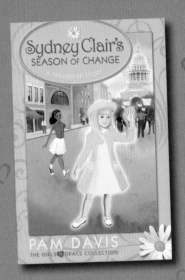

Sydney Clair:
A Girl 'n Grace in the 1960s

Sydney Clair Wilcox is a determined, curious ten-year-old trying to keep up with all the changes around her. The year is 1965, and Penny, her beloved big sister, is moving away to college. In the middle of the civil rights, women's rights, and environmental movements, Sydney Clair's world is changing. Discover how her heart is made ready for the next season of her life and how she prepares for a fragrant friendship that blooms.

Mesi: A Girl 'n Grace in Africa

Mesi (pronounced *Maycee*) is a girl growing up on the continent of Africa. The landscape is as diverse as its people and their beliefs. Mesi's education and her family's well-being are threatened by drought, disease, and war. Yet, amid these hardships, Mesi discovers a God who is near, so near that he cares about what concerns her. Along her journey she finds out about his inexhaustible treasure called grace.

Order online
www.GirlsnGrace.com

I Can Through Christ!®

Girls 'n Grace NIV New Testament

Girls 'n Grace offers an NIV New Testament with an attractive cover to attract this generation of reader. The NIV is the most widely accepted contemporary Bible translation today. This NIV New Testament was created to accurately and faithfully translate the original Greek, Hebrew, and Aramaic biblical texts into clearly understandable English.

Be sure and visit the Girls 'n Grace website for games, quizzes, prizes, and more!

www.GirlsnGrace.com

In Touch with God

 At times we all find ourselves in trouble.

READ ROMANS 3:23–24. God is glorious and without sin. Consider these questions. Is God ever afraid? Does God make mistakes? Does God think only of himself? Are you exactly like God? _____

_____

 When we receive God's mercy and grace, then we can extend mercy and grace to others.

READ EPHESIANS 2:1–3. We all are separated from God's glorious nature because of our sinful nature. Can a perfect God live with sinful people? To answer, consider a clean glass of water. Would it remain pure if one drop of food coloring or some other liquid besides clean water was added?

_____

 When people are unkind it reveals they are poor in God's grace.

READ JOHN 7:38 AND EPHESIANS 2:4–5. Who is God's solution for our sinful nature? _____

_____

 To possess a treasure, you must first seek it.

READ JOHN 3:16–17. Does God love you? Does God want to punish you or save you when you are in trouble? Is that good news?

_____

_____

*Share this book and God's love with a friend, so she can know the love
and grace of God. To learn more about God's inexhaustible treasure of grace,
go to www.GirlsnGrace.com/GraceNow.html*